Just for Girls

special things about me

Alexa Tewkesbury

CWR

Published 2011 by CWR, Waverley Abbey House, Waverley Lane, Farnham, Surrey GU9 8EP, UK. Registered Charity No. 294387. Registered Limited Company No. 1990308. Reprinted 2013.

For list of National Distributors visit www.cwr.org.uk/distributors

Concept development, editing, design and production by CWR
Printed in the UK by Page Bros
ISBN: 978-1-85345-597-1

Hi! We're the Topz Gang

– Topz because we all live at the 'top' of something ... either in houses at the top of the hill, at the top of the flats by the park, even sleeping in a top bunk counts! We are all Christians, and we go to Holly Hill School.

We love Jesus, and try to work out our faith in God in everything we do – at home, at school and with our friends. That even means trying to show God's love to the Dixons Gang who tend to be bullies, and can be a real pain!

If you'd like to know more about us, visit our website at **www.cwr.org.uk/topz** You can read all about us, and how you can get to know and understand the Bible more by reading our *Topz* notes, which are great fun, and written every two months just for you!

Just for Girls

This book is owned by:

_____

I was born on:

_____ (day) _____ (month) _____ (year)

My hair is:

☐ Brown ☐ Blonde ☐ Red ☐ Black

Other _____

My eyes are:

☐ Blue ☐ Green ☐ Brown ☐ Grey

Other _____

I look like this:
(Draw yourself here)

Who's Who in Your Family?

How many sisters do you have? _____

How many girl cousins do you have? _____

How many brothers do you have? _____

How many boy cousins do you have? _____

Are you a twin? ☐ Yes ☐ No

Write the names of your brothers, sisters and cousins here (if there's just you, write 'It's just me and I'm amazing!'):

_____

_____

_____

_____

_____

_____

_____

I've got a brother called John and we're twins. There are two pets in our family, as well. Here are their pictures. Unmuddle the letters underneath to find their names, then put the right name under the right pet.

— — — — —
FRFGU

— — — — —
CUSAY

Are there any pets in your family? ☐ Yes ☐ No

If yes, write down their names and what animals they are. If no, write down an animal you'd like to have and choose a name.

_____

_____

Important Birthdays to Remember

I have a special book in which I write down the birthday dates of all my friends and family. It really helps me remember them. Write down the birthdays of people who are important to you:

Name: **Birthday:**

_____   _____

_____   _____

_____   _____

_____   _____

_____   _____

_____   _____

_____   _____

_____   _____

_____   _____

_____   _____

Birthday Present Ideas

It's easy getting a birthday present for Sarah – she loves anything soft and cuddly! But sometimes choosing presents can be quite difficult. Think of people you might buy a birthday present for and write down here what you think they'd like. Then, next time it's their birthday, you can look back at your list for some present inspiration!

Name: **Possible present:**

Topz Secret Factz About You

What's your favourite ...?

	Josie's	Yours
Colour	Orange	_____
Breakfast cereal	Nutty cornflakes	_____
Weather	Sun, sun and more sun!	_____
Jam	Plum	_____
Bible story	Esther in the Old Testament	_____
Animal	Love them all!	_____
Biscuit	Choc chip cookies	_____
Daydream	Flying to the moon in a hot-air balloon	_____
Shop	Pet shop	_____

What would be your favourite ways to spend a Saturday ...?

Watching TV ☐ Yes ☐ No

Horse riding ☐ Yes ☐ No

Cycling ☐ Yes ☐ No

With friends ☐ Yes ☐ No

Doing homework ☐ Yes ☐ No

Walking the dog (yours or someone else's if you haven't got one) ☐ Yes ☐ No

Tidying your room ☐ Yes ☐ No

Ice skating ☐ Yes ☐ No

Other _____

More Topz Secret Factz About You

What's your yuckiest ...?

	Sarah's	Yours
Insect	cockroach	_____
Vegetable	cauliflower	_____
Ice cream flavour	egg and bacon	_____
Sweet	popping candy	_____
Fruit	grapefruit	_____
Sandwich filling	egg	_____
Subject at school	Maths	_____
Colour	brown	_____
Fizzy drink	dandelion and burdock	_____

Write down five things you've done that you're REALLY PLEASED about:

1 _____

_____

_____

2 _____

_____

_____

3 _____

_____

_____

4 _____

_____

_____

5 _____

_____

_____

School's Cool

What are your TOPZ five favourite things about your school?

Josie's	Yours
1 Seeing Sarah every day	_____
	_____
2 Music lessons	_____
	_____
3 Mufti day	_____
	_____
4 Christmas play	_____
	_____
5 Friday afternoon drama	_____
	_____

I love art, too!

I love sitting next to Josie!

Your Ultimate School Uniform

Supposing you could design the ULTIMATE uniform for the children at your school. What would be your idea of the COOLEST school kit around? Draw Sarah and Josie wearing it here:

Ways to Worship

Play days are the best! Days to do what you want, when you want, with who you want! If you have a REALLY FANTASMAGORICAL time doing something, remember to thank your Father God. God will always be with you through good times *and* bad times – so find special moments to worship Him.

GUESS WHAT ...?
There are 150 psalms in the Old Testament in the Bible. The psalm writers ask questions, cry out to God, worship Him and praise Him.

Topz have written the first few lines of their own psalm of praise to worship God. Think of some things you'd like to praise and thank God for, then add some lines of your own.

Praise God for each new day!
Praise Him for being near me
From when I wake up in the morning
To when I go to sleep at night.
Praise Him for His love
And for family and friends who love me, too.

_____

_____

_____

_____

_____

_____

_____

_____

_____

_____

_____

PRAISE THE LORD!

Here are some ways to enjoy worshipping God:

singing   praying   waving flags

dancing   reading the Bible   playing music

Can you find them in the word search?

S	G	A	L	F	G	N	I	V	A	W	P	R
I	G	Q	S	Q	Y	Q	O	Y	Y	L	D	E
L	M	N	S	E	Q	M	A	I	A	E	W	A
R	K	W	I	Q	J	V	K	Y	V	G	R	D
J	P	E	Q	G	C	G	I	T	S	J	G	I
B	V	H	N	K	N	N	K	A	F	N	O	N
V	T	U	F	I	G	I	N	G	R	H	B	G
Z	B	M	Y	M	N	Z	S	B	H	P	G	T
Q	N	A	U	W	I	B	C	X	K	J	R	H
N	R	S	X	R	C	J	F	J	P	S	E	E
P	I	T	U	C	N	S	D	H	Y	D	A	B
C	C	L	L	W	A	Y	M	W	A	D	B	I
Y	T	Q	Q	I	D	Y	C	E	F	H	M	B
F	N	W	Q	X	Q	E	Y	L	S	F	M	L
S	P	J	Z	P	Z	B	K	B	U	H	Z	E

(Answers on page 117.)

What's in Your Wardrobe ...?

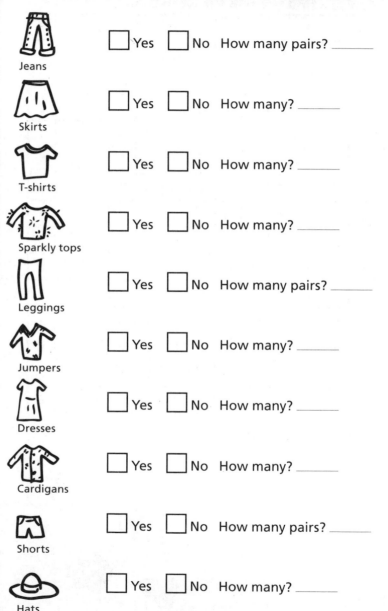

Jeans ☐ Yes ☐ No How many pairs? _____

Skirts ☐ Yes ☐ No How many? _____

T-shirts ☐ Yes ☐ No How many? _____

Sparkly tops ☐ Yes ☐ No How many? _____

Leggings ☐ Yes ☐ No How many pairs? _____

Jumpers ☐ Yes ☐ No How many? _____

Dresses ☐ Yes ☐ No How many? _____

Cardigans ☐ Yes ☐ No How many? _____

Shorts ☐ Yes ☐ No How many pairs? _____

Hats ☐ Yes ☐ No How many? _____

My favourite clothes are the ones that make me feel comfy and warm in winter, and comfy and cool in summer – smart enough in case anyone drops in, but groovy enough in case Topz invite me to the park. I love jeans and jumpers, shorts and T-shirts. How about you?

Which are your favourite clothes?

_____

_____

Draw yourself in your favourite outfit here:

Alike or Not Alike?

Pick a friend you think you know REALLY well, then answer the following questions to find out how ALIKE or NOT ALIKE you are.

What hairstyle do you both have?

Me _____   My friend _____

What books do you like?

Me _____   My friend _____

_____   _____

_____   _____

What's your favourite TV programme?

Me _____   My friend _____

What's your favourite colour?

Me _____   My friend _____

Your favourite biscuits?

Me _____   My friend _____

What ice cream would you choose?

Me _____ My friend _____

**Do you wear the same sort of clothes?
What do you like to wear?**

Me _____ My friend _____

What kind of music do you especially like?

Me _____ My friend _____

What pet do you have or would you choose?

Me _____ My friend _____

What would you both like to spend a Saturday doing?

Me _____ My friend _____

So, how ALIKE or NOT ALIKE are you? You may be VERY alike, or you may seem to like different things – but what's most important is that you clearly LIKE EACH OTHER!

Be a Fashion Designer!

Here's your chance to design an outfit for someone special! Make sure you know them REALLY well, and use the questions to help you decide what kind of clothes they'd enjoy wearing the most.

What's their favourite colour?

_____

What sort of clothes are they most likely to wear – jeans, skirts or dresses?

_____

Do they like wearing T-shirts?

☐ Yes ☐ No

Do they wear more jumpers or more cardigans?

_____

Do they ever wear hats?

☐ Yes ☐ No

Do they like clothes with patterns, pictures or logos, or do they prefer clothes in plain colours?

_____

Do they wear more clothes with zips or more clothes with buttons?

_____

Do they like hoodie-type tops?

☐ Yes ☐ No

What kind of footwear do they wear most – shoes, sandals, flip flops, trainers or boots?

_____

Be a Fashion Designer (continued)!

Do they like wearing accessories, for example scarves, necklaces or bracelets?

☐ Yes ☐ No

Which accessories have you seen them wearing or what do you think would suit them?

_____

_____

Do they ever wear hair accessories?

☐ Yes ☐ No

If yes, make a list of what they wear, for example slides, combs or bands. You could add other hair accessories you think would suit them.

_____

_____

Got all your answers? Now you can use them to design the PERFECT OUTFIT for your friend. Draw them wearing it here. Don't forget to include the footwear and accessories you think would make your friend look SUPER COOL.

How Much Do You Know About Jesus?

Do the quiz and find out! (Answers on page 117.)

1 What was the name of the town where Jesus was born?

☐ Galilee ☐ Blackpool ☐ Bethlehem

2 Where did Jesus grow up?

☐ Nazareth ☐ Jerusalem ☐ Norwich

3 When Jesus was 12, His parents thought they'd lost Him in Jerusalem. Where did they find Him?

☐ In the library ☐ In the Temple ☐ In a shop

4 How old was Jesus when He began His special teaching and healing work for God?

☐ About 30 ☐ About 12 ☐ About 18

5 How many days did Jesus spend fasting and praying in the desert?

☐ 20 ☐ 30 ☐ 40

6 When Jesus went to a wedding in Cana, what did He change water into?

☐ Lemonade ☐ Tea ☐ Wine

7 What did Jesus do when He was on a boat with His disciples and they were caught in a storm?

☐ Swim to shore ☐ Calm the bad weather

☐ Check the weather forecast

8 What kind of stories did Jesus tell to teach people about God?

☐ Parables ☐ Fairy tales ☐ Bedtime stories

9 When Jesus met Zaccheus, the tax collector, what did He say to him?

☐ 'I'm not talking to someone like you.'

☐ 'Go away.' ☐ 'I must stay in your house today.'

10 After Jesus died, how many days was it before He came back to life?

☐ 10 ☐ 3 ☐ 1

TOPZ 10s

Josie's foster cousin, Gabby, is coming to stay for two days at half term. Josie's made a list of the TOPZ five things they could do each day, but TOPZ ten would be even better. Can you come up with another five ideas and add them to the list?

DAY ONE

1 Go for a walk after breakfast.

2 Make chocolate cup cakes for a midnight feast later.

3 Watch a film on DVD.

4 Both write down 20 books we've read, and then compare lists.

5 Have a midnight feast to include chocolate cup cakes (obviously) and ice cream DEFINITELY.

What can you add to make the list up to TOPZ ten?

6 _____

_____

_____

7 _____

_____

_____

8 _____

_____

_____

9 _____

_____

_____

10 _____

_____

_____

Sounds like a wicked day!

Another Topz 10 for Gabby!

Now for DAY TWO!

Here's Josie's TOPZ five:

1 Have a bit of a lie-in due to EXTREME tiredness following midnight feast, but with plenty of chatting if we're awake early.

2 Hair experiment session – see how many different hair-dos we can come up with for each other and take photos of each one.

3 Write a story together taking turns to make up a sentence each.

4 Make puppets with ice lolly sticks and bits of material from Mum's scrap bag.

5 Rehearse and put on a puppet show based on made-up story.

Wow! Josie's very good at this! What can you come up with to make her groovy TOPZ five into a SNAZZY TOPZ ten?

6 _____

_____

_____

7 _____

_____

_____

8 _____

_____

_____

9 _____

_____

_____

10 _____

_____

_____

Super snazzy! Thanks!

Topz Crazy Questions from the Gang

Are YOU ready with your TOPZ crazy answers ...

Have you ever swum with dolphins?

☐ Yes ☐ No ☐ Put on 'must do' list

Have you ever wished you were tiny enough to swim with goldfish?

☐ Yes ☐ No ☐ That's just silly!

Have you ever hiccupped REALLY loudly in a REALLY quiet room?

☐ Yes ☐ No ☐ I know someone who has

Have you ever tried to count the hairs on your head?

☐ Yes ☐ No ☐ Must make time to

Have you ever walked around all day with your shoes on the wrong feet?

☐ Yes ☐ No ☐ I know someone who has

Have you ever ACCIDENTALLY eaten a Brussels sprout?

☐ Yes ☐ No ☐ Must remember to watch out

Have you ever kissed a snail?

☐ Yes ☐ No ☐ Must try to see if handsome prince

Have you ever been in a car and pretended you were in a flying saucer?

☐ Yes ☐ No ☐ Didn't need to pretend

Have you ever walked to school backwards?

☐ Yes ☐ No ☐ I've hopped to school backwards

Have you ever forgotten your own name?

☐ Yes ☐ No ☐ Can't remember

Have you ever ended up at the dentist when you thought you were being taken to the cinema?

☐ Yes ☐ No ☐ Make sure that never happens

Let Your Light Shine

Jesus said, '... your light must shine before people, so that they will see the good things you do and praise your Father in heaven' (Matthew 5 v 16).

God wants everyone everywhere to know how much He loves them and wants them to be a part of His family – and it's up to God's friends to TELL them! We also need to SHOW them by the way we live our lives. That's what Jesus means by letting your light shine. He wants people to notice us!

One way of showing God's love to others is by trying to be kind and helpful, not selfish or rude. It's not always easy. Everyone has grumpy days. I have lots, but then I do have to live with my brother, John, and he's very annoying, so it's not surprising.

Unmuddle the letters below to find different ways to 'let your light shine'. Then write one way in each candle. (Words unmuddled for you on page 117.)

(a) akesp dilnky   **(b) rheas**
(c) leph uot   **(d) mofcort**
(e) eb a efrdni

Friends Forever!

No doubt about it, Josie and Sarah will be friends forever. When they grow up, they want to work together, too. Here's a list of their ideas for starting up a business. Which ones do you think they'd be good at?

- [ ] Animal rescue centre
- [ ] Zoo
- [ ] Dog-walking service
- [ ] Cat-sitting for cat owners on holiday
- [ ] Tea rooms
- [ ] Celebration cakes of all shapes and sizes
- [ ] Fashion design
- [ ] Scrumptious sandwich delivery service

- Have you got a best friend you'd like to work with when you're older?

- What ideas do YOU have for a business you could run together?

- Think of the things you both enjoy and make your own possible business list!

- (If you're not sure who you might like to work with at the moment, make a list anyway and then keep your eyes open for the right person!)

1 _____

2 _____

3 _____

4 _____

5 _____

6 _____

7 _____

8 _____

Could YOU be a
TV SCRIPT WRITER? (1)

Do you love reading?
Ever thought you might like to be a writer?
What about a writer who gets their stories
brought to life on TV?

Why not have a go at writing your own script! If you know what TV you like watching, it'll help you decide what kind of programme you might like to create. Use these questions to get you started:

What are your favourite TV programmes?

_____

_____

_____

_____

_____

Are you more interested in ...?

☐ Comedies ☐ Dramas ☐ Don't mind

Do you prefer ...?

☐ Cartoons ☐ Live action (actors) ☐ Don't mind

Would you rather watch ...?

☐ One-off episodes where each story is complete (series)

☐ Continuing stories where you have to wait for the next episode to find out what happens (serials)

☐ Don't mind

How long do you like TV programmes to last (for example 30 minutes)?

_____

Who are your favourite TV actors and actresses?

_____

_____

_____

_____

_____

Could YOU be a
TV SCRIPT WRITER? (2)

Time to get thinking!

If you wrote a script would it be for a drama or a comedy?

Here are some possible plot starter ideas:

- Girl tries to win a place at a theatre school.

- Family has to move to a different area because of mother's new job.

- Two friends decide to run a problem page in a local magazine.

- Someone's kidnapping cats and a brother and sister set out to discover why and who's responsible.

- Group of children launch a campaign to stop their local cinema from being closed down.

- Girl discovers by accident that she can travel through time.

What other plot ideas have you got? Use the list on the previous page, books you've read, or stories from TV programmes you like to inspire you. Remember, if you're going to write a cartoon script, it really can be about ANYTHING ANYWHERE!

_____

_____

_____

_____

_____

Would you like your programme to be a series or a serial?

_____

Is it going to be set in the present, the past or maybe even the future?

_____

Where could your story take place (for example in a big town, in a fairground, on the moon)?

_____

Could YOU be a
TV SCRIPT WRITER? (3)

Once you've chosen a plot, who are the characters to star in your programme?

- Will they be a family or a group of friends?

- What ages will they be? Just children and teenagers? All ages?

- If you've chosen to write for a cartoon, could the main characters be animals or even monsters?

YOU decide ...

List possible characters here:

Name: **Boy/girl/adult/other:**   **Age:**

_____   _____   _____

_____   _____   _____

_____   _____   _____

_____   _____   _____

_____   _____   _____

You've probably read loads of books, but have you ever seen a SCRIPT before? In case you haven't, here's a short scene starring the Topz Gang which shows you how to set out YOUR VERY OWN script.

Topz have just arrived at school in the morning to find that the whole place has disappeared! Honestly, there's just nothing there any more! Read the scene, then flip over the page to practise your own script-writing by adding what you think the Gang might have said next.

SCENE 1. OUTSIDE HOLLY HILL SCHOOL

<u>**SARAH**</u> **(NERVOUSLY)**
OK, this is weird.

<u>**JOHN**</u>
The whole school's vanished! I think it's a bit more than just 'weird'.

<u>**JOSIE**</u>
So what would *you* call it?

(JOHN SHRUGS HIS SHOULDERS.)

<u>**BENNY**</u>
I know what *I'd* call it: megastonkingly weird!

Could YOU be a
TV SCRIPT WRITER? (4)

Can you carry on the conversation? Remember to write the name of the person speaking before you put in what they say.

WHAT HAPPENS NEXT IS UP TO YOU!

_____ (name of person speaking)

_____

_____

_____

_____

_____

_____

_____

_____

_____

_____

_____

Think about the plot for YOUR series or serial and see if you can come up with a catchy title. Now imagine it's been shown on TV and is soon to be out on DVD! Design a DVD cover here, including the title, and make your TV programme look ACEY-JACEY! Can't wait to see it already!

Prayer Power

The way we talk may change because of how we're feeling or what's happening to us. Sarah and Josie have come up with a list of different ways of talking. Unmuddle the letters to see what they are.

We can:

epiwhsr   _ _ _ _ _ _ _

hsuto   _ _ _ _ _

ngaro   _ _ _ _ _

iewhn   _ _ _ _ _

useaql   _ _ _ _ _ _

blrmeug   _ _ _ _ _ _ _

samecr   _ _ _ _ _ _

tutmre   _ _ _ _ _ _

memubl   _ _ _ _ _ _

rltecho   _ _ _ _ _ _ _

Check your unmuddling skills on page 118.

When you talk to God, you can always be completely honest about how you're feeling. If something AWESOME has happened, you can SHOUT out to Him in praise! If you're worried or unhappy about something, you can CRY out to Him for help. Just as talking to friends around you helps build up strong relationships with them, so talking to God helps your relationship with Him grow, too.

What would you like to talk to God (pray) about this week?

MY PRAYER LIST FOR _____
(Today's date)

1 _____

_____

2 _____

_____

3 _____

_____

4 _____

_____

Pray Away!

Answer the questions to help YOUR prayer life be the ABSOLUTE TOPZ! You can check your answers on page 118.

1 Where should you pray?

(a) In church ☐

(b) In your bedroom ☐

(c) Anywhere you feel like it ☐

2 When should you pray?

(a) Once in the morning ☐

(b) Every day whenever you feel like it ☐

(c) Only on Sundays ☐

3 Who does God listen to?

(a) Only church leaders ☐

(b) Only really clever people who can pray using big words ☐

(c) Anyone who wants to talk to Him ☐

4 How should you feel when you talk to God?

(a) You can talk to Him however you feel
– happy or sad, scared or excited, lonely or loved □

(b) You should only talk to Him when you've got
something to say thank you for □

(c) You should only talk to Him if you need
His help □

**5 Talking to God is important, but how does God
talk to His friends?**

(a) Through a loud speaker □

(b) Through the Bible, through talking to other
people, through what's going on in your life □

(c) Over the Internet □

GUESS WHAT ...?
Praying isn't always easy. Even Jesus' twelve special
friends needed Him to help them learn how to talk to
God (read Luke chapter 11 v 1–4). But just remember,
God wants to be involved in YOUR life and He LOVES
to listen to you.

Say 'Thank You' the Arty Way

I love saying 'thank you'. It can really make someone smile. You don't have to wait until you're given a present. You can say 'thank you' to someone for helping you, for taking care of you, or even for cheering you up if you've been feeling sad. Saying 'thank you' is good for YOU because it encourages you to appreciate other people – and it's good for the people you thank because it lets them know that you VALUE them. So, as words go, 'thank you' is a pretty awesome twosome!

Why not make a THANK YOU card for someone?

Sarah wrote this short verse in her card for Josie:

Thanks for being a friend.
You make my life so rosy.
There'll never be another you –
The one and only JOSIE!

Can you write a verse to go in your card?

_____

_____

_____

_____

Now for the arty bit. Use this page to design the picture for the front of your card. When you've got it just right, you can copy it onto some folded paper or cardboard and write your verse inside. For the ultimate finishing touch, write on the back:

Designed by _____ (your name)
exclusively for _____ (the person you're giving the card to).

A Verse a Day ...

Have you heard the old saying, 'An apple a day keeps the doctor away'? Not sure that's completely true – we eat LOADS of apples, but we both still caught tonsillitis and had to swallow spoonfuls of what the doctor called medicine, but we happen to *know* was actually disgusting yellow death juice. Now, learning a Bible verse a day might not keep the doctor away either, but it is a TOPZ way to help you stay close to God and remember His promises.

Here are seven verses for you to memorise. They're all taken from the *Good News Bible*. Try learning one a day for a week with the reference, too (in brackets after each one), so that you know which part of the Bible the verse is from. As you learn them, tick them off!

Day 1: 'You, LORD, give perfect peace ...' (Isaiah 26 v 3) ☐

Day 2: '... God is love.' (1 John 4 v 8) ☐

Day 3: 'And I will be with you always, to the end of the age.' (Matthew 28 v 20) ☐

Day 4: 'Humble yourselves before the Lord, and he will lift you up.' (James 4 v 10) ☐

Day 5: 'Leave all your worries with him, because he cares for you.' (1 Peter 5 v 7)

How are you doing? Only two to go! Why not test yourself by using the verse test over the page?

Day 6: 'God is the same Lord of all and richly blesses all who call to him.' (Romans 10 v 12)

Day 7: '... I will not be afraid, LORD, for you are with me.' (Psalm 23 v 4)

Take the Verse Test!

Fill in the blanks below to see how well you remember your verses. Only look back at the previous page once you've written in the missing words to check you're right.

1 '__ __ __ , LORD, give __ __ __ __ __ __ __

__ __ __ __ __ ...' (Isaiah __ __ v 3)

2 '...__ __ __ is __ __ __ __ .' (__ John 4 v __)

3 'And I will be __ __ __ __   __ __ __

__ __ __ __ __ __ , to the __ __ __ of the __ __ __ .'

(__ __ __ __ __ __ __ 28 v 20)

4 'Humble __ __ __ __ __ __ __ __ __ __ __ before the

__ __ __ __ , and he __ __ __ __   __ __ __ __ you up.'

(James __ v__ __)

5 '__ __ __ __ __ all your __ __ __ __ __ __ __ with him,

because he __ __ __ __ __ __ __ __ you.'

(1 __ __ __ __ __ __ v 7)

6 '__ __ __ is the same __ __ __ __ of all and

__ __ __ __ __ __ __ __ __ __ __ __ __ __ all who

call to him.' (Romans __ __ v __ __)

7 '... I will not be __ __ __ __ __ __ __ , Lᴏʀᴅ, for __ __ __

__ __ __ __ __ __ __ __ __.'

(__ __ __ __ __ __ __ v 4)

Whenever you feel worried or afraid, having snippets of God's Word like these in your head will help you remind yourself of His HUGE and EVERLASTING love for you!

More Topz Crazy Questions from the Gang

Which famous person would you like to write to?

_____

Which famous person would you like to have a letter from?

_____

Have you ever eaten cheese with chocolate?

☐ Yes ☐ No ☐ I'd like to

What other strange combination would you like to try?

_____

Have you ever taken a sheep for a walk?

☐ Yes ☐ No ☐ I'd like to

Have you ever found buried treasure?

☐ Yes ☐ No ☐ I'd like to

Have you ever worn your socks on your ears?

☐ Yes ☐ No ☐ Will give it a try!

Have you ever tried writing your name with the hand you don't usually write with? If not, why not try it now?

_____

Have you ever been bitten by a duck?

☐ Yes ☐ No ☐ Don't plan to be!

Have you ever stayed awake all night reading?

☐ Yes ☐ No ☐ I'd like to

Have you ever lived in a tree house?

☐ Yes ☐ No ☐ I'd like to

How to be a Topz Friend

The Topz Gang are the best of friends – that's:

Benny	John	Danny
Sarah	Josie	Dave
Paul		

Can you find all their names in the word search?

D	A	E	P	Y	T	H	P	E	N	K	L
Y	S	I	U	P	N	A	S	V	Y	V	X
D	Y	S	D	A	U	N	T	A	J	A	C
R	I	O	F	L	O	F	A	D	G	M	D
Y	S	J	B	Y	B	C	R	D	D	R	Z
N	L	Z	N	H	O	J	A	N	E	B	E
N	I	H	G	D	T	C	R	R	H	O	M
E	V	E	C	N	H	C	N	T	Q	R	K
B	Q	Q	W	A	I	M	K	Z	A	P	C
H	E	X	R	U	H	Y	O	K	G	D	G
P	W	A	B	M	F	K	K	J	U	A	O
G	S	O	B	X	E	F	Z	P	X	O	I

(Answer on page 118.)

Jesus said, 'As I have loved you, so you must love one another' (John 13 v 34). Topz do sometimes have fallouts, but they try hard to love each other and be the kind of friends Jesus wants them to be.

What kind of friend does Jesus want you to be?
Crack the code to find three words to describe a good friend and three to describe someone who wouldn't make a very good friend at all! Put a tick against the good and a cross against the not-so-good. Check your code-cracking by looking at the answers on page 118.

+1 = a   ++1 = b   +2 = c   ++2 = d   +3 = e   ++3 = f etc

+6 +5 ++7 ++2

— — — —   ☐

+10 +3 ++6 ++3 +5 +10 ++4

— — — — — — —   ☐

++4 +3 ++6 ++8 ++3 +11 ++6

— — — — — — —   ☐

+5 +7 ++8 +1 ++10 +5 +3 ++7 ++10

— — — — — — — — —   ☐

+11 ++7 +2 +1 ++9 +5 ++7 +4

— — — — — — — —   ☐

++3 +8 ++9 +4 +5 ++11 +5 ++7 +4

— — — — — — — — —   ☐

How to be a Topz Friend (2)

Make a list of five of your best friends and say what you like most about each one:

Name _____

What I like most _____

_____

Name _____

What I like most _____

_____

Name _____

What I like most _____

_____

Name _____

What I like most _____

_____

Name _____

What I like most _____

_____

Try sketching or drawing a fun caricature of your friends here:

Topz 20 Most Spectacular Moments in the World (yet)!

Sarah and Josie have each written down their personal TOPZ five most FANDABULOUS moments in their lives so far. Can you add five of YOUR OWN incredibly TOPZ moments to each list to make a whole TOPZ 20 most spectacular moments in the world (yet):

Sarah's list

1 Being born! (I suppose I don't exactly remember it but, as moments go, it's *got* to have been pretty spectacular!)

2 Asking Jesus into my life.

3 Bringing Saucy home to live with us.

4 When Mrs Allbright found Gruff all safe after he'd been lost for HOURS.

5 The day Mum came home after she'd been away looking after Gran.

Add your TOPZ five moments to Sarah's list to get halfway to TOPZ 20:

6 _____

_____

7 _____

_____

8 _____

_____

9 _____

_____

10 _____

_____

Topz 20 Most Spectacular Moments in the World (yet)!

Only 10 to go for the whole TOPZ 20!

Josie's list

11 When I asked God to be my very best Friend.

12 My foster cousin writing to tell me her biggest secret – what her name is short for. (I can't write it here, obviously, as it's a secret.)

13 When Sarah came up with the awesomely awesome name 'Life Starts Here' for our groovy-doovy church drama group.

14 Getting better from tonsillitis and being able to swallow things like cake again without it REALLY hurting – and if you've had tonsillitis like Sarah and me, you'll know exactly what I'm talking about!

15 Playing violin in a school concert and getting all the notes right.

Write another five of your TOPZ moments here:

16 _____

_____

17 _____

_____

18 _____

_____

19 _____

_____

20 _____

_____

YAAYY! You did it – TOPZ 20! Keep this book incredibly safe and, next time things don't seem to be going so well, read through your SPECTACULAR moments to remind yourself of God's amazing blessings.

Car Boot

Greg, the youth leader at Topz's church, is doing a car boot sale to raise money for the local homeless centre. Lots of people have brought things for him to sell and Topz are going to help out on the day of the sale.

Here's a list of what Greg's collected so far:

books	saucepans	radio
toys	clock	vase
candle holder	cushions	skateboard
fishing rod	mugs	DVDs

Can you find all these in the word search?

H	L	L	E	B	T	O	V	F	G	R	V
C	A	N	D	L	E	H	O	L	D	E	R
F	M	M	V	S	K	T	O	Y	S	D	O
A	I	A	U	C	K	W	Z	A	K	V	I
C	S	S	O	G	Z	O	U	R	A	D	D
E	T	L	H	S	S	C	O	W	T	S	A
G	C	P	O	I	E	I	V	B	E	Z	R
E	O	I	J	P	N	X	W	B	B	O	F
P	F	H	A	R	M	G	Z	A	O	R	Z
F	D	N	B	B	N	A	R	H	A	A	D
X	S	N	V	N	P	G	N	O	R	X	L
S	N	O	I	H	S	U	C	C	D	X	D

(Answer on page 119.)

Look at the picture of Greg's car boot full of the items in the word search. There's one thing from the list missing. When you've spotted what it is, draw it in. (Answer on page 119.)

Raising money for groups of people or animals who really need it is a brilliant way to spend some of your time. If you helped to organise a charity car boot sale, is there a special charity you'd like to give the money to? If yes, write the name here:

Ways to Raise!

Car boot sales aren't the only way to raise money for charities or people who need special help. What other ways can you think of?

There are also lots of charity shops around. They sell things given to them by people who no longer want or need them. These might be clothes, books, CDs, DVDs, toys and shoes. All the money raised from sales goes to the charity each shop supports. Perhaps you have something in a cupboard or drawer that you no longer use or wear. If so, why not help someone else by finding a charity shop to give it to?

Here are some things Topz found in their cupboards that they are going to take to a charity shop. Who do you think is going to give what? Match them up by drawing a line linking the Gang member with the item.

(Answers on page 119.)

Parable in Pictures

Here is the parable Jesus told about a woman who lost a silver coin. Back then, silver coins would have been EXTREMELY precious, so it's no wonder she is so upset. In the following pictures, all the coins are missing. Read the story and draw them in.

There was once a woman who had ten silver coins. But one day, she realised one coin was missing …

Straightaway, she lit a lamp and began to search for it.

Draw the nine coins in a pile here ↑

It's got to be here somewhere.

... she looked in every nook and cranny ...

She swept the floor ...

Parable in Pictures (continued)

... until finally ...

She picked the coin up happily and gave it a polish.

In fact, the woman was so excited to have all ten coins again that she invited her friends and neighbours to a big celebration party!

Draw the ten coins and lots of balloons

Jesus told this parable to explain to people how much God loves them. Just as the woman was upset over her precious, lost coin – then over the moon when she found it – so God is sad that there are people who haven't made friends with Him yet, and aren't a part of His family. So whenever someone new does give their life to God, there is a HUGE party in heaven to celebrate: they were lost, but now they're found!

You can read Jesus' parable about the lost coin in the Bible in the book of Luke chapter 15 and verses 8–10.

Party-Time (1)

If, like the woman in the lost coin story, you've got something to celebrate, why not plan a party? It could be for you or perhaps for someone else. Use these pages to get some ideas together. Then, when it's time for a party … it's party-time!

What's your party going to celebrate?

Birthday ☐

Christmas ☐

Finding that shoe you lost months ago ☐

End of term ☐

Your best friend coming back from holiday ☐

Welcome home ☐

Your cat's first birthday ☐

Moving house ☐

Other (describe) _____

What kind of party?

Outdoors ☐

Indoors ☐

Smart dress ☐

Casual dress ☐

Fancy dress ☐

Themed (for example film or book characters) ☐

If themed, what theme ideas do you have?

_____

_____

_____

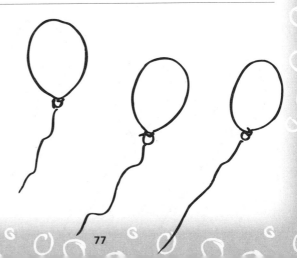

Party-Time (2)

What games will you play? For example:

Pass the parcel ☐

Musical chairs ☐

Charades ☐

Apple bobbing ☐

Treasure hunt ☐

Invent a dance ☐

Other game ideas:

_____

_____

_____

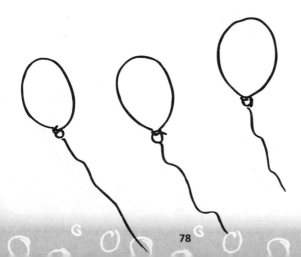

Very important party bit – WHAT YOU'RE GOING TO EAT! Make a list of the food you'd serve at your party. Include all the details, for example sandwich fillings, pizza toppings, ice cream and cake flavours.

Even if your party isn't for a birthday, it's still super-cool to have a BIG cake! Draw your ULTIMATE celebration cake here – and don't forget to save a piece for me!

Create Your Dream Bedroom

When Sarah was ill, to cheer her up, Josie helped her decide how she could give her bedroom a makeover.

What's your bedroom like? Is it big? Is it small? Is it perfect for you already? Why not have a go at designing YOUR ULTIMATE DREAM bedroom? If yours really is exactly the way you like it and you wouldn't change a thing, imagine you're creating a super-duper bedroom for your best friend.

Bedroom colour?

_____

Painted walls or wallpaper?

_____

If wallpaper – plain or patterned?

_____

What sort of pictures on the walls (for example family and pet photos, posters of favourite TV characters)?

_____

_____

Curtain colour?

_____

Plain curtains or patterned?

_____

Carpet colour?

_____

Fluffy rug on floor beside bed for extra comfort on bare feet when getting up in the morning?

☐ Yes   ☐ No

If yes, rug colour?

_____

More Bedroom Dreams ...

Tick which furniture:

Chest of drawers ☐

Dressing table with mirror ☐

Walk-in wardrobe (remember this would also be very groovy for hiding in) ☐

Desk (for doing things like homework or filling in this Secret Diary) ☐

To relax on: Comfy chair ☐

Squidgy beanbag ☐

Both ☐

Bookcase complete with favourite books ☐

Radio/CD player on top of bookcase ☐

Four-poster bed ☐

Ordinary bed ☐

Because the bed in any bedroom is a BIG piece of furniture, it's important that the covers look just right – especially in a DREAM bedroom. Think of a gorgeous picture or pattern and draw here exactly the sort of duvet cover you'd like to wake up under:

FANTASMAGORICAL!
Can we come and stay soon?!

Design-a-mag (1)

Imagine being the editor of your very own magazine! That means YOU'RE IN CHARGE. You can plan it, choose exactly what goes into it, and even decide on the way you'd like it to look. Benny is the editor of the Sunday Club magazine at his church and he says it's –

Stonking!

Have a go! Start a plan for your very own magazine here:

Do you ever read any magazines or comics? If so, what do you like about them (for example stories (fiction), jokes, interviews with famous people)?

_____

_____

_____

_____

_____

_____

Would you like your magazine to be for ...?

☐ Girls ☐ Boys ☐ Both

What would you like to include in your magazine?

○ Real life stories ☐ Yes ☐ No

○ Fashion pages ☐ Yes ☐ No

○ Book reviews ☐ Yes ☐ No

○ Film reviews ☐ Yes ☐ No

○ Music news ☐ Yes ☐ No

○ Celebrity interviews ☐ Yes ☐ No

○ Advertisements ☐ Yes ☐ No

○ Cartoons ☐ Yes ☐ No

○ Letters page ☐ Yes ☐ No

○ Sport ☐ Yes ☐ No

○ Puzzle/quiz page ☐ Yes ☐ No

Put them in order of your favourite type of pages by numbering them from 1–11 in the circles.

Design-a-mag (2)

I love reading about books and films in magazines. Sometimes I don't know what to read or what to watch, but reading about a really good book or film gives me ideas and helps me to make up my mind.

What books could you write a review for to include in your magazine? Remember to put the authors' names, too.

_____

_____

_____

_____

What films would you like to write about?

_____

_____

_____

_____

Who would you interview? You could choose famous people, or maybe you could interview your best friend. (Come to think of it, your best friend might be famous!)

Cartoons in magazines are BRILLIANT! I've read loads of funny stories written in cartoon style. And the characters can be REALLY weird. Think of two characters for a cartoon story and draw them here. They can be people or animals – or even talking carrots! You can draw what you like in a cartoon!

Design-a-mag (3)

Lots of magazines begin with a 'Letter from the Editor' on the first page. This is usually all about what's coming up inside. Once you've decided what you'd like to go in your FIRST magazine, have a go at writing an editor's letter to your readers so they know exactly what's in store:

HELLO READERS!

Wow! Your magazine sounds fandabulous!

Now you need a name for your magazine. What are you going to call it?

_____

Some magazine names are designed to look really eye-catching on the front cover. The name of Benny's Sunday Club magazine looks like this:

Turn your magazine's name into a fun design that'll make EVERYONE want to read what's inside:

God's Instruction Book

The Bible is BRILLIANT! Not only does it teach us about God and His Son, Jesus, it also gives us instructions for how to live our lives in the way that's best. The FABBIEST part is that they're GOD'S OWN INSTRUCTIONS! And He should definitely know what *is* the best for us – after all, He knows us inside out and back to front because He made us.

How well do you think you know the Bible? Do the quiz and find out! (When you've finished, check your answers on page 119.)

1 God told Noah to build an ark to save himself from:

☐ A hurricane ☐ A flood

☐ A whale ☐ The Loch Ness Monster

2 Daniel was thrown into a pit. What was in it?

☐ Sharks ☐ Snakes

☐ Snails ☐ Lions

3 The first thing God created was light. What did He create next?

- [ ] TV
- [ ] Birds
- [ ] Sky
- [ ] The wheel

4 David fought a giant man called:

- [ ] Joseph
- [ ] Samuel
- [ ] The BFG
- [ ] Goliath

5 In the Old Testament, what special present did Joseph's father give him?

- [ ] A coat of many colours
- [ ] A PS3
- [ ] A pair of sandals
- [ ] A puppy

6 What was Jacob's twin brother called?

- [ ] John
- [ ] Esau
- [ ] Daniel
- [ ] Abraham

More Bible Quizzing!

7 What did Hannah beg God for?

☐ A bike   ☐ A kitten

☐ A baby sister   ☐ A son

8 What is the last book of the Old Testament called?

☐ The book of Exodus

☐ The book of Revelation

☐ The book of Malachi

☐ The book of Cooking

9 What's the first book of the New Testament called?

☐ The book of Mark

☐ The book of Flowers

☐ The book of Chocolate Cakes

☐ The book of Matthew

10 When Jesus was born, why were Mary and Joseph in Bethlehem?

☐ For a football match   ☐ To be counted

☐ To go to hospital   ☐ For a holiday

11 How did the shepherds know Jesus had been born?

☐ Heard it on *The News*   ☐ Saw it in the paper

☐ Told by an angel   ☐ Overheard gossip

12 How many people does Jesus feed with five loaves of bread and two fishes?

☐ Over five thousand   ☐ Five hundred

☐ Fifty   ☐ Twelve

13 Peter was one of Jesus' disciples. What was his job?

☐ Teacher   ☐ Shopkeeper

☐ Fisherman   ☐ Children's entertainer

14 Who did Jesus first speak to after He was raised from the dead?

☐ Mary Magdalen   ☐ A gardener

☐ An angel   ☐ A policeman

You – Ten Years On ...

It's easy to imagine yourself as you'll be tomorrow or this time next week. But can you guess what you and your life might be like in TEN YEARS' TIME?

How old will you be?

_____

How tall will you be?

_____

What will your hairstyle be like?

_____

What sort of clothes will you be wearing?

_____

Will you wear jewellery?

_____

Where will you be living?

_____

Will you have any pets? If so, what will you have?

_____

Will you have a job or will you be at college or university?

_____

If you have a job, what will you be doing?

_____

Who will be your friends?

_____

What will you enjoy doing in your spare time?

_____

More Ten Years On ...

What sort of books will you enjoy reading (for example funny books, real life stories)?

_____

What sort of programmes will you watch on TV?

_____

Will you play any sport? If so, what will you play?

_____

Where will you go on holiday?

_____

What time will you go to bed?

_____

What will you do at weekends?

_____

Now draw your future self here in the sort of clothes you think you might be wearing – TEN YEARS ON …

Topz 10s Stuck in a Bus

Here are Sarah and Josie's TOPZ five things to think about when stuck in a broken-down school bus – which they were last week.

Can you add five more to each list so that next time the bus breaks down, Sarah and Josie will still have plenty to keep their minds busy?

Sarah's stuck-in-a-bus things to think about

1 How many hours a week does Saucy spend sleeping?

2 If John were a cat, would we still argue?

3 If John were a cat, would he look silly with sticky-up ears?

4 If I were a cat, would Saucy like me?

5 If I were a cat, would I still be allowed chocolate? In fact, would I even *like* chocolate? (Don't be silly, of course I would.)

Add your five things to think about to make a TOPZ ten – because when buses, or cars, break down, you just really need to have thinking stuff ... don't you ...?

6 _____

_____

7 _____

_____

8 _____

_____

9 _____

_____

10 _____

_____

Still Stuck in a Bus!

Josie's stuck-in-a-bus (or car) things to think about

1 If football had never been invented, would boys still want to run around kicking things? If boys had never been invented, would we ever have needed foot deodorisers?

2 If you kissed a frog, would it really turn into a handsome prince, or would it just make your lips all slimy?

3 If a frog kissed you, would you turn into a frog?

4 If umbrellas could talk, would they say, 'How come you only ever take me out when it's raining?'

5 If bees were the size of birds, how much more honey would they be able to make? And, assuming it's loads more, would there be enough glass jars to put it in? And would all the people in the world be able to eat enough toast to use it up … or would there be a honey flood …?

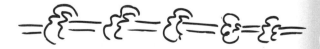

Another wacky five things to think about, please! Will yours be wackier than mine?

6 _____

_____

7 _____

_____

8 _____

_____

9 _____

_____

10 _____

_____

Even *More* Topz
Crazy Questions

Have you ever fallen down a rabbit hole?

☐ Yes   ☐ No   ☐ I know someone who has

Have you ever eaten an apple with your hands behind your back?

☐ Yes   ☐ No   ☐ Must give that a go

Have you ever drawn a picture with your eyes closed?

☐ Yes   ☐ No   If no, why not try it here?

Have you ever stroked a hedgehog?

☐ Yes   ☐ No   ☐ Ow! Not sure I want to!

Have you ever tickled an elephant with a toothbrush?

☐ Yes ☐ No ☐ Take toothbrush on next visit to zoo

Have you ever had a staring contest with a cat?

☐ Yes ☐ No ☐ I know someone who has

Have you ever hidden someone else's sunglasses in rice pudding?

☐ Yes ☐ No ☐ I found some in rice pudding once

Have you ever tried knitting with spaghetti?

☐ Yes ☐ No ☐ Must ask a knitter if they have

Have you ever seen a chicken ice-skating?

☐ Yes ☐ No ☐ I've never seen a chicken

Have you ever walked more than 15 miles in a day?

☐ Yes ☐ No ☐ I know someone who has

Have you ever built a raft and sailed on it?

☐ Yes ☐ No ☐ Must find out how to build one

Have you ever built a tower of marshmallows?

☐ Yes ☐ No ☐ Yum! Must try

The Big Topz Interview

The Bible tells us all about Jesus' marvellous miracles. He turned water into wine; He made sick people well; He brought dead people back to life; *and* He fed more than 5,000 people with just five loaves of barley bread and two fishes!

The huge crowd of over 5,000 people had come to catch a glimpse of Jesus and to hear Him teaching about God. At the end of the day, Jesus' disciples were worried. 'You need to send them away, Jesus. They'll be hungry and they need to go and find food.'

But Jesus just smiled. Jesus knew that His heavenly Father could make a little bit go a long, long way. When a small boy gave the only food he had with him to Jesus – five loaves and two fishes – Jesus told His disciples to share it out between the 5,000 people. And, when they did, miraculously there was enough for everyone! Too much, in fact, because when all the leftovers were picked up, they filled twelve baskets!

That's my favourite Bible story! It shows how much God cares for people, because He didn't want them to have to go home hungry. It shows what INCREDIBLE things He can do by His power. And it also shows what amazing stuff can happen when you put your trust in Him the way the boy did when he gave Jesus his food!

Topz want you to imagine that YOU are the child in that Bible story. Just think about that special day. How awesome it must have felt to be the ONE PERSON who had something Jesus could use to work a miracle!

Now, YOU are going to star in THE BIG TOPZ INTERVIEW! Answer the questions as if YOU were that faithful child with the picnic ...

So, tell us how it was waking up on the morning of the miracle. How did you feel about going to listen to Jesus teaching?

_____

_____

_____

Was it your own idea to pack a picnic?

_____

Did you buy the food on the way to listen to Jesus or did you bring it from home?

_____

The Big Topz Interview

How long did it take you to walk to where Jesus was going to be?

_____

What was the weather like?

_____

Did you go with anyone else or were you on your own?

_____

Was this the first time you'd seen Jesus?

_____

How did it feel to see Him in person?

_____

_____

_____

Five thousand people is an awful lot! Was it a bit scary being in such a huge crowd?

_____

What did you think when Jesus' disciples came round asking everyone if they had any food? Were you worried about giving yours to Jesus in case you then had to walk all the way home without having anything to eat yourself?

_____

_____

_____

What was it like knowing that Jesus had worked a miracle with YOUR picnic?

_____

As days go, how would you score that miracle day out of ten?

_____

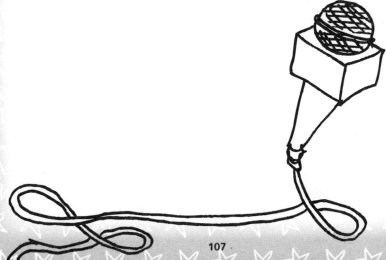

Backwards and Forwards

If you could travel back in time 200 years, what would you take with you to show people there how we live now?

Topz would take:

Paul	computer	**You** _____
Sarah	hairdryer	**You** _____
Dave	mobile phone	**You** _____
John	television	**You** _____
Josie	CD player	**You** _____
Danny	electric toothbrush	**You** _____
Benny	skateboard	**You** _____

What about travelling forward 200 years? By then, people might be living very differently from the way we do now. What would you take to show them that they might not have anymore?

Topz would take:

Josie	books	**You**	
Danny	bicycle	**You**	
Benny	sandwich	**You**	
Dave	tin of baked beans	**You**	
Sarah	umbrella	**You**	
Paul	glasses (the kind that help you see	**You**	
John	tent	**You**	

Topz Time Travelling

Of course, if you're thinking about travelling forwards and backwards in time, you're going to need a TIME MACHINE.

Answer the questions to help you come up with a design for the most incredibly TOPZ time machine the world has ever seen!

What colour would you like your time machine to be?

_____

Would you like there to be an 'invisibility' button you could press to make your time machine invisible? Then no one would be able to see you travelling through time.

☐ Yes ☐ No

How big should your time machine be? (This will depend on how many friends you are taking with you on your adventures.)

☐ Large ☐ Medium ☐ Small

Will your time machine make lots of noise or will it travel silently?

_____

What will you call your time machine?

_____

Can you picture your time machine in your head? Topz can't wait to see it! Draw it here:

Pray and Praise

One of the best ways we can use our mouths is to praise our heavenly Father! He is with us every day, He forgives us for the wrong things we do the moment we ask Him to, He is there to talk to when we're happy and when we're sad, His love for us goes on and on – He's just the absolute TOPZ!

I praise You, Lord, for fab friends – especially Josie.

Dear God, thank You for Mum and Dad. They're cool!

You know me inside out. Wow, Lord, You're amazing!

I praise You, Father, for forgiving me when I get things wrong.

I know You'll never leave me. Thank You, Lord.

Lord, I praise You for football. It's super-stonking!

Thank You, God, for making me fast when I run.

Here's a list of things you could praise God for right now. **Find them in the word search, then thank Him for all the different ways He cares for you**.

Jesus
food
friends
clothes

love
family
home

moonlight
holidays
sunshine

H	Y	U	A	O	V	J	V	R	F	G	S
P	O	M	O	O	N	L	I	G	H	T	U
Y	R	L	S	V	Z	J	F	E	V	E	N
Y	L	T	I	L	B	R	D	R	V	S	S
I	P	I	K	D	I	F	O	O	D	U	H
L	P	E	M	E	A	R	L	C	T	S	I
T	Z	F	N	A	N	Y	H	N	W	E	N
A	U	D	Z	Z	F	O	S	O	Y	J	E
I	S	E	H	T	O	L	C	S	M	H	G
D	M	U	N	D	Z	U	L	O	V	E	K
I	I	E	S	I	T	C	O	I	N	R	J
L	S	R	R	U	H	L	K	Z	Q	T	V

(Answer on page 120.)

Faith Every Day

When everything is going well, praising God and putting your faith in Him probably seem easy to do. But when you feel unhappy or worried or scared about something, it can seem a lot harder to trust that He will always be there to listen to you and help you. However you are feeling, remember that **GOD IS LOVE** – and His love for you is never-ending.

Opposite are some special words to say whenever you need to remind yourself that God is your

VERY BEST FRIEND

who only wants the

VERY BEST FOR YOU

See if you can learn them by heart so you can repeat them wherever you are, whenever you need to. You can tick each one off as you memorise it.

I am special to God every day. ☐

God is always ready to forgive me when I tell Him I'm sorry. ☐

God will always answer my prayers. ☐

God loves having me as His friend. ☐

God always keeps His promises. ☐

God knows me inside out because He made me. ☐

How much does God love me? More than there are stars in the sky! ☐

ANSWERS

Page 19

S	G	A	L	F	G	N	I	V	A	W	P	R
I	G	Q	S	Q	Y	Q	O	Y	Y	L	D	E
L	M	N	S	E	Q	M	A	I	A	E	W	A
R	K	W	I	Q	J	V	K	Y	V	G	R	D
J	P	E	Q	G	C	G	I	T	S	J	G	I
B	V	H	N	K	N	N	K	A	F	N	O	N
V	T	U	F	I	G	I	N	G	R	H	B	G
Z	B	M	Y	M	N	Z	S	B	H	P	G	T
Q	N	A	U	W	I	B	C	X	K	J	R	H
N	R	S	X	R	C	J	F	J	P	S	E	E
P	I	T	U	C	N	S	D	H	Y	D	A	B
C	C	L	L	W	A	Y	M	W	A	D	B	I
Y	T	Q	Q	I	D	Y	C	E	F	H	M	B
F	N	W	Q	X	Q	E	Y	L	S	F	M	L
S	P	J	Z	P	Z	B	K	B	U	H	Z	E

Pages 28–29

1	Bethlehem	**7**	Calm the bad weather
2	Nazareth	**8**	Parables
3	In the Temple	**9**	'I must stay in your
4	About 30		house today.'
5	40	**10**	3
6	Wine		

Page 37

(a) speak kindly **(b)** share **(c)** help out **(d)** comfort
(e) be a friend

Page 48

whisper; shout; groan; whine; squeal; grumble; scream; mutter; mumble; chortle

Pages 50–51

1 (c) **2** (b) **3** (c) **4** (a) **5** (b)

Page 60

D	A	E	P	Y	T	H	P	E	N	K	L
Y	S	I	U	P	N	A	S	V	Y	V	X
D	Y	S	D	A	U	N	T	A	J	A	C
R	I	O	F	L	O	F	A	D	G	M	D
Y	S	J	B	Y	B	C	R	D	D	R	Z
N	L	Z	N	H	O	J	A	N	E	B	E
N	I	H	G	D	T	C	R	R	H	O	M
E	V	E	C	N	H	C	N	T	Q	R	K
B	Q	Q	W	A	I	M	K	Z	A	P	C
H	E	X	R	U	H	Y	O	K	G	D	G
P	W	A	B	M	F	K	K	J	U	A	O
G	S	O	B	X	E	F	Z	P	X	O	I

Page 61

✔ kind ✘ selfish ✔ helpful
✘ impatient ✘ uncaring ✔ forgiving

Page 68

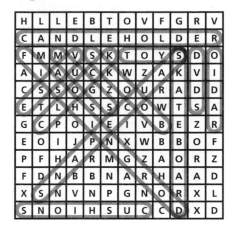

Page 69
Missing Item
The clock

Page 71
Sarah – cuddly cat toy

Josie – 'Easy Exercises For The Violin' DVD

Paul – computer game

John – 'How To Train Your Puppy' DVD

Dave – bicycle lamp

Benny – football

Danny – running shoes

Pages 91–93

1 A flood
2 Lions
3 Sky
4 Goliath
5 A coat of many colours
6 Esau
7 A son

8 The Book of Malachi
9 The Book of Matthew
10 To be counted
11 Told by an angel
12 Over five thousand
13 Fisherman
14 Mary Magdalen

Page 113

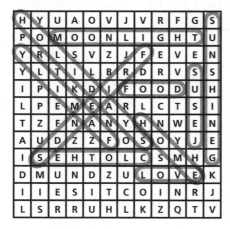

Other Topz Diaries for you to enjoy

These special editions of *Topz Secret Diaries* will help you discover things about yourself and God with questions and quizzes, engaging puzzles, word searches, doodles, lists to write and more.

**Topz Secret Diaries:
Boys Only**
ISBN: 978-1-85345-596-4

**Topz Secret Diaries:
Christmas Cracker**
ISBN: 978-1-85345-993-1

Benny's Barmy Bits
ISBN: 978-1-85345-431-8

Danny's Daring Days
ISBN: 978-1-85345-502-5

Dave's Dizzy Doodles
ISBN: 978-1-85345-552-0

**Gruff & Saucy's
Topzy-Turvy Tales**
ISBN: 978-1-85345-553-7

John's Jam-Packed Jottings
ISBN: 978-1-85345-503-2

Josie's Jazzy Journal
ISBN: 978-1-85345-457-8

Paul's Potty Pages
ISBN: 978-1-85345-456-1

Sarah's Secret Scribblings
ISBN: 978-1-85345-432-5

Go to **www.cwr.org.uk/store**,
call 01252 784700
or visit a Christian bookshop.

For correct prices visit **www.cwr.org.uk/topzbooks**

Let the Topz Gang guide you through the Bible

With the *Topz Guide to the Bible* you'll discover the exciting story of the Old Testament from start to finish, learn what the world was like in Jesus' day, and find out what each book in the Bible is about.

And the Topz Gang will make it fun all the way with their usual blend of colourful illustrations, cartoons, word games, puzzles and lively writing. This is the perfect way for 7- to 11-year-olds to get to know their Bibles.

ISBN:
978-1-85345-313-7

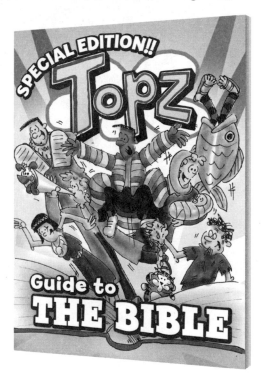

Topz for New Christians

Thirty days of Bible notes to help you find faith in Jesus and have fun exploring your new life with Him.

ISBN: 978-1-85345-104-1

Go to **www.cwr.org.uk/topzbooks** call 01252 784700 or visit a Christian bookshop.

For correct prices visit **www.cwr.org.uk/topzbooks**

Topz is a colourful daily devotional for 7- to 11-year-olds.

In each issue the Topz Gang teach children biblical truths through word games, puzzles, riddles, cartoons, competitions, simple prayers and daily Bible readings.

Available as an annual subscription
(6 bimonthly issues includes p&p)
or as single issues.

Go to **www.cwr.org.uk/topzeveryday**
call 01252 784700 or visit a Christian bookshop.

For correct prices visit **www.cwr.org.uk/topzeveryday**